# DOING HER BIT

## A Story About the Woman's Land Army of America

Erin Hagar • *Illustrated by* Jen Hill

ini Charlesbridge

With gratitude to Elaine Weiss and to Vermont College of Fine Arts

—E. H.

For all the Helens who've inspired me to dream bigger, go farther, and smile brighter

—J. H.

WWI posters front endsheets: Library of Congress, Prints & Photographs Division
Photographs back endsheets: National Photo Company Collection and Harris and Ewing Collection,
    both through the Library of Congress

Published by Charlesbridge
85 Main Street • Watertown, MA 02472
(617) 926-0329 • www.charlesbridge.com

**Library of Congress Cataloging-in-Publication Data**
Hagar, Erin, author.
    Doing her bit: a story about the Woman's Land Army of America/Erin Hagar; illustrated by Jen Hill.
       pages cm
    Summary: Helen wants to contribute to the war effort after the United States goes to war in 1917—
so she joins the Woman's Land Army of America, an organization that trains women to do farm work,
replacing the workers drafted into the army. Includes bibliographical references.
    ISBN 978-1-58089-646-7 (reinforced for library use)
    ISBN 978-1-60734-872-6 (ebook)
    ISBN 978-1-60734-873-3 (ebook pdf)
1. Woman's Land Army of America—Juvenile fiction. 2. World War, 1914–1918—United States—
Juvenile fiction. 3. World War, 1914–1918—Women—New York (State)—Juvenile fiction. 4. Agricultural
laborers—New York (State)—Juvenile fiction. 5. Farm life—New York (State)—History—Juvenile fiction.
6. New York (State)—History—Juvenile fiction. [1. Woman's Land Army of America—Fiction. 2. World
War, 1914–1918—United States—Fiction. 3. World War, 1914–1918—Women—Fiction. 4. Agricultural
laborers—Fiction. 5. Farm life—New York (State)—History—Fiction. 6. New York (State)—History—
Fiction.] I. Hill, Jen, 1975– illustrator. II. Title.

PZ7.1.H23Do 2016
813.6—dc23
[Fic]    2015026779

Printed in China
(hc) 10 9 8 7 6 5 4 3 2 1

Illustrations painted in gouache and Adobe Photoshop
Display type set in Madrid by Rabbit Reproductions Typefoundry
Text type set in ITC Goudy Sans by Bitstream Inc.
Color separations by Colourscan Print Co Pte Ltd, Singapore
Printed by 1010 Printing International Limited in Huizhou, Guangdong, China
Production supervision by Brian G. Walker
Designed by Whitney Leader-Picone and Diane M. Earley

Helen Stevens was a New York City college girl. She'd never pitched hay or milked a cow. And she'd certainly never worn men's overalls. But it was 1917, and there was a war on.

Helen rolled bandages and knit socks for soldiers headed overseas. But she wanted something more—to do her bit. Yes, indeed, she wanted an adventure.

One day, Helen saw a sign that took root in her heart.

At Helen's farewell luncheon, her father said,
"Woman's Land Army—craziest thing I ever heard.
No farmer in his right mind would hire you girls."

Helen looked right at him. "They'll have to. With
so many men working in factories or training to fight,
who else will bring in the crops?"

"All that sun and dirt," Helen's mother said with a sigh. "Take good care of your hands. There will be dances in the fall."

Helen swished her hand in the air as if she were swatting a pesky fly. "I'll be fine," she said.

Helen headed north to the Women's Agricultural Camp in Bedford, New York, on a sunny day in June. Lots of women were already there. They were ready to learn about farming—ready to work.

Folks called them the "farmerettes." The name fit
perfectly. But the overalls? Well, those were another story.

A stern-looking woman entered the dining tent after breakfast the next morning. She stood tall and solid as she looked the farmerettes over with eyes like stones. Everything about her made Helen think of rock.

"My name is Ida Ogilvie," the woman said. "I'm the director of this camp. Farmers aren't sure you can do this work. It's my job to see that you can. Let's begin."

Ida showed them how to whitewash the dairy and
build a fence around the chicken coop. Helen found out
that potatoes don't grow on trees, and Alice discovered
the difference between a bean plant and bindweed. Even
Harriet, who'd grown up on a farm, learned new skills.
She'd never been allowed to plow before.

Yes, indeed, they learned a lot.

But not one farmer came by to hire them.

The days got harder. In the training garden, Helen worked her hoe until a huge blister bubbled on the palm of her hand.

*Surely Ida will let me rest until this heals*, Helen thought.

No, ma'am. Ida soaked that blister in vinegar until Helen's eyes teared up from the sting.

"There," Ida said. "That'll clean it out and toughen the skin." She wrapped Helen's hand in a bandage and sent her back to work.

Blisters turned into calluses, and muscles got stronger. Still, no farmers would hire them.

One day, while Helen was weeding the tomatoes, a huge black snake wriggled right in front of her. In a flash, she jumped up, grabbed her hoe, and killed that snake dead!

Helen was quite pleased with herself.

But Ida wasn't.

"Never kill a snake," she scolded. "Snakes help farmers. They eat animals that ruin crops."

Helen was sweaty, hungry, and tired. Every muscle ached.

"Maybe snakes help farmers, but we surely don't!" She waved her arm around. "Not one farmer will hire us!"

Ida stood like a boulder, her back to the hot sun. "Come with me," she said. "Alice and Harriet, you come, too."

*What have I done?* Helen wondered.

Ida marched them all to the rickety Model T they'd nicknamed Henry. Henry was like a stubborn mule—he moved only when he wanted to.

They drove nine miles until they passed a sign
that read "Davie's Farm."

They saw a farmer alone in his field. For a moment, Ida hesitated. Then she set her chiseled jaw, lifted her skirts, and marched right up to him. Helen, Harriet, and Alice followed close behind.

"Mr. Davie," Ida said, "I know you need help. In only two weeks, these young women have learned to plow and plant and seed and weed. They can mend fences, milk cows, whitewash a dairy, and drive a tractor. Will you hire them, sir?"

Farmer Davie wiped his hands on his overalls and spat into the dirt.

"I heard your girls expect men's wages," he said.

Ida turned to Helen, Alice, and Harriet. "Would you work tomorrow for free to show Mr. Davie what you can do?"

Helen nodded. Alice and Harriet did, too.

"Be here at seven," Farmer Davie said, "ready to work."

On the ride home, Helen looked at Ida and thought about the kind of rocks that sparkle when you crack them open.

Helen, Alice, and Harriet loaded their tools and lunch pails into Henry early the next morning.

Halfway to the farm, a rake tumbled out of the car. And then stubborn old Henry wouldn't start up again. They cranked the engine, but Henry only sputtered and hissed.

*No!* Helen thought. *We can't be late!*

"Harriet, take the wheel," Helen ordered. "Alice, let's push!"

They pushed that car until the engine caught, and they scrambled back in. Nothing would keep them from working.

The sun beat down and sweat ran down, and the farmerettes worked. Helen had never smelled anything as nasty as a turnip plant, but she thinned them out without a fuss. When a black snake slithered between her boots, she let it be. She was a farmerette, and nothing would stop her from doing her bit.

At the end of the day, Farmer Davie looked around
and let out a long, slow whistle.

"Not bad. But what about when I need help with
the livestock? Come back tomorrow and show me
you can work with animals. Then I'll decide about
hiring you on."

*Another day with no pay?*

Helen dug her boots into that hard, packed earth. Men's work deserved men's wages.

"We're trained with livestock, too," Helen said. "If you want us back tomorrow, it'll be two dollars a day for each of us."

Farmer Davie rubbed his toe in the dirt. "All right. Bring two more girls with you. Got a field of cabbages that'll rot if we don't get 'em in."

Back at camp, Helen, Alice, and Harriet buzzed like honeybees as they told Ida about their day. They rounded up two more women to work for Farmer Davie and danced to tunes they played on the Victrola. Ida watched with a quiet smile.

Helen woke the next morning to another long day in Farmer Davie's fields. And she worked hard. They all did.

Potatoes and tomatoes, berries and beets—all summer long. The days got shorter and the nights got crisp. Apples ripened in the orchard. Soon, it would be time to head home. But the adventure of being a farmerette had sprouted in Helen's heart. If her country still needed her, she would come back to these fields. Yes, indeed, she'd do her bit all over again.